SMOKE SIGNALS

SMOKE SIGNALS

ROSELYN OGDEN MILLER

authorHOUSE®

AuthorHouse™
1663 Liberty Drive
Bloomington, IN 47403
www.authorhouse.com
Phone: 1-800-839-8640

Published by AuthorHouse 09/30/2015

ISBN: 978-1-4969-1132-2 (sc)
ISBN: 978-1-4969-1141-4 (e)

Print information available on the last page.

Any people depicted in stock imagery provided by Thinkstock are models,
and such images are being used for illustrative purposes only.
Certain stock imagery © Thinkstock.

This book is printed on acid-free paper.

DEDICATIONS

To my husband

He'To Hune Hakek'at Sni.

(Translation from Phoebe Tallman)

To my former grade school class mate, Jeanie Long, who saw the same dream I did and helped me stay on track with the correctness of the Lakota culture and getting the story written.

This story is written in memory of all men and women who have fought to save our country to continue to live on the principals of our forefathers.

CONTENTS

CODE NEVER BROKEN

"Class settle down, please, we have lots of work to do. Did everyone get a drink?" When the children had settled themselves, Miss Gorman turned to the flag hanging at the front of the class room. The children stood quietly and placed their hands over their hearts and pledged their allegiance to America, sang 'God Bless America', then sat quietly in their desks.

Miss Gorman turned to face them and said, "Take your history notebooks and pencils out of your desks as we are going to start the day with our history lesson. This is the quarter we study the wars in which the United States have fought. We are going to concentrate on World War II. Your assignment will be to write an essay on one of the battles or other events that took place during that war. Before I assign each of your topics, we have a guest speaker to start off the project, our principal, Mr. Grayson."

A tall slender man walked through the doorway and to the front of the room.

"Thank you, Miss Gorman. Boys and girls you are going to begin to study one of the most interesting histories of our United States, World War II. I love the stories of the way our men and women gave their lives to keep our world free so you could grow up and enjoy that freedom. But what really fascinates me is the way all people, no matter what race or religion, color or creed came together and served. Not only did the men and women serve in the military but men, women and the children here in the United States were busy, too, supporting their service men and women. What we want you to focus on is how your ancestors, the American Indians, especially the Lakota, served not only in the military but also on the home front. How many of you had family members serve in that war."

One hand slowly raised but soon dropped when no one else volunteered.

'Yes, Isaiah, you raised your hand. Who in your family served?" asked Mr. Grayson.

"I think my grandmother's brother was in communications," said Isaiah rather timidly.

"I'm not surprised you don't know for sure as it happened about 60 years ago, which makes anyone who joined any branch of the military would now be 80 years or older, like your great grandparents. Billy Jack, you and Betty have a great grandfather living nearby, don't you? Ishmael, I think your great grandfather served. Anyway, some of you have a great resource sitting on your front door step so take advantage of it when working on the assignment Miss Gorman is going to give you. Some grandparents may not want to talk about it or remember much about it. If you do find someone with a story to share, encourage them, Maybe they just need a little prodding or interest shown so visit with them anyway. They may know or remember more than they think. Study and enjoy what you learn. I will read each of your essays Miss Gorman plans for you to write at the end of this quarter history. Anyone of you can come to see me if you feel the need."

BILLY JACK'S DISAPPOINTMENT

Billy Jack waited for Miss Gorman to explain the new assignment, he remembered the school news Mama had read in the parents booklet for this year to he and his sister, Betty. Mama had always loved school and wanted her children to love it too.

When Mama read to him about some of the battles of World War II, he was quite intrigued by the battle of Dunkirk. Mama had once helped the son of a friend look up information about it and he knew that finding the information and writing it down wouldn't take long at all. It was really was interesting how all those little boats had rescued so many men from being drowned or captured. Boy, he hoped he got that assignment and be the one chosen to write about it. The Battle of Dunkirk! Boy, he could hardly wait for Miss Gorman to begin telling them what they had to report on. He crossed his fingers as he waited.

"Class, as Mr. Grayson said we will study World War II. At the completion of the unit each pupil will write a 75 word essay on the subject I assign you. Remember when we do essays the words '*the, and, but*' and '*or*' are not to be counted. Also, you do your research in the history books, encyclopedias, and computers. I know we haven't had much time to learn how the computers work best, but I'm sure I can help. I want you to learn about your heritage from the original source if possible, not what your parents may have remembered hearing."

"Tommy, you will write on the battle of Midway, Jerome the battle of Iwo Jima and Isaiah the Battle of Dunkirk. Now …" Miss Gorman's voice droned on but Billy Jack didn't hear it. All he could hear was 'Isaiah…Battle of the Dunkirk…Isaiah Battle of the Dunkirk…"

"Billy Jack did you hear what I assigned you to write your essay on?" asked Miss Gorman.

"Uh, yeah, I mean. Yes, Ma'am …I'm sorry Miss Gorman I didn't hear you."

"I didn't think so. Billy Jack, you are to write about the communications of the service men in battles." She moved to the next student. "Jericho, you are to write about the food and how they got it to the men and served it.…"

Billy Jack sat stunned. Communications. Communications!!

How could anybody write seventy-five words on the two-way radio?

Billy Jack was so glad when he heard the last bell of the day ring and school was dismissed. He had not been able to concentrate and was called down in nearly every class for not paying attention.

As he began walking rapidly to the bus, Isaiah came running up to him.

"Billy Jack, you lucky duck. You get to write about communications. I get stuck with a battle. I admit it was an interesting battle but I would rather…"

Billy Jack turned around and just spit his words out.

4

"'Communications!' Did you hear that? You're the one who knows about communications so why didn't you get it?"

Isaiah stopped short and stared at his best friend. Billy Jack walked right past Isaiah and got on the bus, went clear to the back, squeezed between Fredrick and Joe leaving no room for Isaiah to sit with him.

SEARCHING FOR INFORMATION

"Betty, wait for me," cried Ginger running toward Betty as she made her way to the school bus.

"Well, hurry up, Ginger, or the bus will leave without me," replied Betty.

"Don't worry. I just left Dad's office and the bus driver was in there," Ginger hastened to report, nearly out of breath.

"Oh, okay, but I can't wait to start looking up information for the history paper Miss Gorman assigned us."

"That's what I want to talk to you about. I know our history books and the computer have information on World War II but where do we find information about the Lakota people? I mean you can ask your mom and dad. I…I can't. I'm not of Indian descent and I…well, I don't know what to do. I don't have anyone to ask. Does the computer tell stories of the various nationalities of the people who served such as the Lakota? I mean . . .You can talk to your parents and your Two Gramps but…"

Betty laughed. "Two Gramps? What would he know about the war? He is old."

"It's just that Dad mentioned him when he spoke to the class. Like he knew something about your Two Gramps," said Ginger. "I just moved here when Dad was assigned to this school to fill in as a principal 'til a new one can be hired. You'd be surprised all the schools I've been to because of Dad's job. You've been my best friend since we moved here so I…thought I'd ask you. Can you help me?" begged Ginger.

"Sure I'll be glad to help but I can hardly wait to start looking up what the women did in the war. What is your subject?"

"What did the people do here in America to help the men and women who were fighting overseas?" read Ginger from her notebook. "I'm not even sure I know what that means. Do you?"

"No, but…Oh, no! Here comes Mr. Fast Wolf. I gotta run. Ask your dad. I'll see if mom understands what Miss Gorman means. See you Monday," she said as Mr. Fast Wolf shooed her up the steps into the bus.

Still angry about not getting the assignment he wanted, Billy Jack wandered into the kitchen where his sister Betty sat at the table. She had her history book open and note paper beside it to take notes for her essay. Billy Jack walked up to the table watched her a few minutes and then taking his hand he scattered her neat pile of papers all across the table, brushing some to the floor.

"Billy Jack, stop that!! Mama!!" cried Betty as she watched her brother. Suddenly he grabbed her school book and threw it to the floor.

"Mama!! Make Billy Jack stop."

"Young man what are you doing?" exclaimed Mama as she walked into the kitchen in time to see her ten year old son throw the school book to the floor.

"Get yourself down there and pick it up, then straighten up those papers you scattered." She watched as he picked up the papers and book, straightened the papers and handed them to his sister. He then sat quietly knowing his mother was not through with him.

"First apologize to your sister and then tell me what this is all about."

"I'm sorry, Betty," muttered Billy Jack.

"Louder, Billy Jack, and say it like you mean it," said Mama in a no nonsense voice.

"I'm sorry, Betty, I'm just so mad." said Billy Jack in a strong voice.

"Thank you son, now, what are you so angry about?"

Billy Jack sat at the table and just shrugged his shoulders.

"Something must be wrong. So tell me." encouraged his mother.

Betty sat as quietly as she could then said, "We have to write essay about World War II. Billy Jack wanted The Battle of Dunkirk but Miss Gorman gave it to Isaiah. He was mean to Isaiah, too. Wouldn't let him sit by him on the bus and..."

"Excuse me young lady, I believe your name is Betty and your brother's name is Billy Jack," stated Mother again in her no nonsense voice.

Betty ducked her head. "Yes, Mama," she said and opened her book again.

Billy placed his hands on the oilcloth that covered the table top, shrugged his shoulders again.

The look on his mother's face warned him he had better speak and do it quickly.

"Okay!! Miss Gorman said for our history class, instead of just reading about World War II like the other 4ᵗʰ graders classes have in the past we have to write a 75 word essay about it. All the boys got to write about a battle. I had read about the Battle of Dunkirk I thought it was a cool story. So I was hoping I would get it to write my essay on it. But no, Miss Gorman gave that battle to Isaiah," said Billy Jack nearly out of breath after that long and indignant report.

"Yeah, and Billy Jack was given communications," said helpful Betty.

"Elizabeth Johanna, I thought I made myself clear this is between Billy Jack and myself."

"Yes, Mama, but doesn't Billy Jack have to apologize to Isaiah? It wasn't Isaiah's fault Miss Gorman gave Billy Jack communications to write about instead of a battle. And Isaiah gets to write about the battle of Dunkirk that Billy Jack wanted."

"Betty," Mama said in an exasperated voice. "But, you're right. He will apologize to Isaiah."

"Communications, of all things. Our history book says they had two-way radios."

"What about code talkers? Wasn't there a movie about code talkers? Your dad watched it and he said they played an important part in America winning the war," said Mama.

"Ya, but Dad said they were all Navaho!"

"Can't you use that information?"

"I can, Mama, but the essays are to include what our Lakota people did in the war," said Billy Jack before Betty could volunteer any more information about his reaction to the assignment.

"Billy Jack, Two Gramps was in World War II. Maybe he can help you with your assignment," encouraged Mama.

"He's old and forgetful. What would he remember? He probably even got to be at the Battle of Dunkirk. Man, it makes me mad I didn't get that topic. I bet Isaiah is laughing his fool head off, 'cause he knew I wanted it," scorned Billy Jack.

Mama turned when she heard the screen door snap shut behind her.

"Oh, hi, Isaiah, I didn't hear you knock," said Mama as Billy Jack's best friend came into the kitchen.

"I knocked but you were all too busy to answer, so I just came in. I hope it's alright, you always tell me to make myself at home," explained Isaiah.

Mama had to smile. Isaiah was such a nice boy. Never made any trouble and was polite. She saw Billy Jack quietly stand up and start walking toward his bedroom.

"Billy Jack, you come back here. Isaiah is here to play with you," Mama exclaimed.

"It's all right Mrs. Bladen. I think he is mad at me but I don't know why. Why are you acting like you are mad at me Billy Jack? What did I do to you?" asked Isaiah.

"Don't act like you don't know why I'm mad! You knew I wanted to write about the Battle of Dunkirk and you got it. I got COMMUNICATIONS!!" Billy Jack yelled. "What was so important about the men talking each other, other than having to whisper so the enemy didn't hear them," he said scornfully.

"Well, don't feel so noble. I wanted communications because my Grandma's brother was in communications and he was a code talker. I wanted to write about him. What do I know about the Battle of

Dunkirk? It was probably just like all the other battles," snapped Isaiah before he ran out of the room. The Bladen family heard the door slam. They all sat with their mouths wide open in surprise. They had never seen Isaiah angry before.

Billy Jack came to his senses first. "Did he say his great uncle was a code talker? Isaiah is Lakota isn't he, so wouldn't his grandpa be Lakota, Mama?" he asked. "I thought only the Navaho were code talkers."

"Isaiah, wait," called Billy Jack as he ran out the door. He couldn't see his friend anywhere. He ran toward Isaiah's house hoping to catch him outside. Isaiah's grandmother was ill so Billy Jack had never been in her home where Isaiah probably was now. He hesitated to knock on the door. He stood there hoping Isaiah would see him and come out.

***

"Well, that was quite a shock," said Mama as she recovered her senses. "If all the boys were assigned the battles what were the girls' assignments, Betty?"

BETTY LOOKS FOR ANCESTORS

"Mama, not all the boys were assigned battles. Jericho has to write about what the soldiers had to eat and how they got the food to them. And I," said Betty importantly, "get to write about the women who served in the army and navy. Do you know anything about Lakota women serving, Mama? Were they nurses or did the men have to be nurses?"

"What does the encyclopedia or the history books say?"

"Not much," replied Betty frowning. "Mama, why do the books only tell about what the men do? Aren't women just as important? Just like Two Gramps taking Billy Jack to the old camping grounds and telling the old stories, but when I asked to go he said no. Why, Mama. I'd like to hear the old stories, too. But no, I can't go. I can only go with the women and make flowers for graves or help make quilts."

"Betty, women are important in their own way. Who would give men their sons to carry on the traditions; or gather and preserve the food as well as cook their daily meals; or make and decorate their ceremonial clothes for their remembered history; tend the crops; or the many other things we women do for everyone's survival. The quilts and flowers are to honor our people. While we are creating flowers we are remembering the person whose grave it will be placed on. The memories warm us and make us laugh or cry. They make us feel the goodness that surrounds us. The quilts not only warms the person it is given to but it warms the receiver's heart to think they are important enough in the women's lives that they would take the time to create it just for them. We Lakota love giving. These acts just enhance the love we feel for one another," explained Mama.

"Oh, I never thought of it that way. But someday I will hear the stories of the men," she said slyly.

Suddenly she remembered Ginger. "Mama, you know my new friend, Ginger? She isn't Indian and she has to write about what the people of the United States did to help with the war effort. Do you know anything about that?"

"Not really," said Mama. "I don't know of many of our people who knew about the men and women in that war. I guess you are going to have to just ask anyone you know what they know or remember hearing about it. Most of those service people aren't alive any more. I do know that our people here in South Dakota had no way of finding out what was going on overseas or anywhere else. The majority of us didn't have radios or television or computers. Few got the newspapers."

"Mama we are to talk only to the people who are old like Two Gramps because Mr. Grayson said that is what age they would be now. Besides, Mama, television and computers were not even invented yet back then," exclaimed Betty.

"I know, I was just teasing you. Have you found anything on the computer at school? Or in your dad's old history books?"

"Not much," sighed Betty.

Billy Jack came into the house, his head hung down. "I wish I hadn't been so mean to Isaiah," he said again.

"Did you get a chance to apologize to him?" asked mama.

"No, he went into his grandma's house. She is very sick you know, so I never go in there. I didn't know his great uncle was a code talker. In fact I'm not even sure I know what a code talker is," he admitted. "Darn, I wish I had known about his uncle."

"Why? So you could ask him about it for your report? That doesn't sound like a friend to me," said Betty.

"Billy Jack, the mailman just dropped off the mail. There is another letter for Two Gramps from the U.S. government. I hope it isn't serious. Why don't you take it over to him and remind him tonight is his night for sharing our supper," said Mama.

Later Two Gramps came shuffling along side Billy Jack. His head bowed as though he had to watch his feet to make sure they didn't suddenly go the wrong way.

He greeted his grand-daughter in law in the Lakota tongue and smiled at his great granddaughter.

"Come, sit, Two Gramps. John is working late at the hospital so we will eat without him. Did Billy Jack give you the letter from the government?" asked Mama.

"Yes. I just put it up with the other one I got a couple of months ago. They probably want me to go back to the war again. I think I'm too old," said Two Gramps.

"You mean you haven't read either one? Two Gramps you can't ignore the government. Can Billy Jack go get them and we can look at them with you after supper? Or would you rather wait until John is here?" asked Mama.

"You can read as well as John can, can't you, Daughter?"

"Well, yes, I can. It's just I thought it might be something official and he would understand better than I would," she said.

"Go get the letters, Billy Jack. They are on the second shelf of the bookshelves," instructed Two Gramps.

Billy Jack was out of the house in a flash and soon returned holding up two official looking envelopes. "Are these the ones, Two Gramps?" he asked waving them in front of Two Gramps' face.

"Yes. Give them to your *Ita*."

Mama carefully took a table knife and slit the envelopes open one at a time cautiously, almost gently. Then unfolding the first one she held it out to Two Gramps.

"You read it, Daughter, I seem to have left my spectacles at home," he said with a grin.

Mama looked at the official looking letter and gasped.

"Two Gramps," she said, "it is a letter telling you, you are to be honored for serving as a code talker in World War II!!"

"World War II? Why, Daughter that was 60, 65 years ago. Has the letter been lost?"

Mama looked at the date on the letter and said, "No, it is this year." She glanced at Billy Jack as he suddenly stood on his chair raised his arms to the ceiling and let out a yell. Then he folded his hands under his chin and bowed his head. "Thank you," he whispered.

"Billy Jack, sit down before you fall down," scolded Mama.

Billy Jack sat down and turned to his Two Gramps. "Why didn't you ever talk about it, Two Gramps?"

"Why didn't you ever ask?" retorted Two Gramps his grin back again.

"Well, I'm asking now," said Billy Jack, 'cause I have to write a paper on communication during the second World War and all I could find on internet was the stories of the Navaho code talkers. You aren't a Navaho are you?" he asked excitedly.

"Billy Jack, calm down and let me see what the second letter is about." said Mama.

TWO GRAMPS IS CELEBRATED

The door opened. Billy Jack and Betty's father came in. "What is all the excitement about? I could hear you clear out in the street," exclaimed Dad.

"Two Gramps served in World War II..." began Billy Jack.

"He was a code talker and he isn't Navaho!" exclaimed Betty.

Dad looked at Mama. "Elizabeth can you make some sense of this for me? I know he served in the Second World War and I know he isn't Navaho. He's Lakota like the rest of us, but why is everyone so excited?"

Billy Jack started to speak again but his father put his hands on the boy's shoulders and Billy Jack sat quietly while his mother explained.

"A few months ago Two Gramps got a letter from the government. Then today he got another one."

"I didn't open them. I thought they wanted me to go back into war and I'm too old for that. But Elizabeth thought I should open them so I let her," Two Gramps explained to his grandson.

Elizabeth held out the official looking letters to her husband. "I would have waited 'til you got home but I thought you were on call so I read one of them for him."

"Dr. Steel came back earlier than he anticipated so I could leave," explained dad as he read the document.

He turned to his grandfather. "You have had this knowledge for nearly 70 years yet I've never heard you speak of it. In fact, I didn't know there were Indians using their own language for the code words until I saw that movie that just came out. And like Billy Jack said only the Navaho were ever mentioned. Why was that?"

"We were sworn to silence. What good would it do to have a secret code if everybody and their dog knew it? They didn't know how long they would be able to use the code, so we just promised and forgot about it. I don't know why they are telling about it now," said Two Gramps.

Billy Jack looked at his father.

"You have a question for Two Gramps, Billy Jack?"

"Yes sir."

"Two Gramps, if they are having a celebration for you that means it's not a secret anymore, right?"

"I would guess I can talk about it now. Why?" asked Two Gramps. "It's just old war stories. Nothing you would be interested in."

"But I am," cried Billy Jack. "I know I didn't listen to your other war stories but now I will!!"

"We have to write an essay on World War II. The assignment is to include stories of our ancestors' part in the war and Billy Jack is to write about communications. You should have heard him, Two Gramps, when he was told he had to write about 'communications'. He nearly took the roof off the house he was so mad. He wanted the Battle of Dunkirk but Isaiah got that battle. I get to write about the women who served."

"Did you know any women in the army or navy, Two Gramps?" asked Betty.

"Don't be silly, Betty. Women weren't allowed in the Army or Navy," scorned Billy Jack.

"Hold it young man," said Two Gramps. "Lots of women served in the war right here at home and overseas. And, yes, they were in the army and navy. Two of our Lakota women were in the Women's Army Corps and one of them was a pilot."

"What!" All four of his grandchildren sat up and took notice.

"Who was it, Two Gramps," asked Betty as she ran to get her note book. "Wait 'til I get my paper and pencil."

Two Gramps waited then said, "Since it is your lesson I think you need to look it up in your books and if you don't find it I'm sure Mrs. Little Deer can help you. Now if you don't mind I will go home. I've had a long day."

"Excuse me, Two Gramps, may I ask you one question?" asked Billy Jack.

"If you make it snappy, I'm an old man and I need my sleep," replied Two Gramps as he held the kitchen door open.

"My friend Isaiah said his great uncle was a code talker. Is he right and did you know him?" asked Billy Jack.

"That's two questions. Yes, he was and yes, I knew him. He was my cousin and partner. Good night."

The family sat stunned as they thought about what Two Gramps said.

"Did Two Gramps leave his letters here?" asked Dad.

"Yes, but it is private mail, isn't it?" asked Billy Jack remembering Mama's rule about reading other people's mail.

"It is but in this case I think it is alright to read it." said Dad. He took the letters out of their envelopes and said, "Listen to this."

The Department of Interior

"The people of the United States wish to Honor

Cpl WILLIAM JOHNSON BLADEN for his valiant military service as SECRET CODE TALKER during America's conflict with foreign countries in the past. A special day honoring your valiant defense will be held in the near future. Please plan to grace us with your presence. More information will be following.
Sincerely in the honor of your country.

Hezekiah Horst

Hezekiah Horst.

"I thought his name was Two Gramps," exclaimed Billy Jack. "Oh, yeah, his name is just like mine, William Johnson Bladen. Did they call him Billy Jack like me? When he was little, I mean."

"No," replied dad. "He was called Will. The letter that came today must be the invitation. Do you think he will want to go?"

"I don't know," said Mama. "I wish your dad was alive, he could talk him into it. Did you know he was a code talker, John?"

"I heard Dad ask him about it but he didn't have much to say. I think the fact his cousin was killed during battle was something he didn't want to remember so he just shut it out of his mind."

"Dad, I have to do a report on the code talkers of World War II for a history report. Do you think Two Gramps will talk to me about it? 'Cause that's who Miss Gorman wants us to talk to for our essays," said Billy Jack.

"I don't know, son. All you can do is ask him. But if he doesn't you'll just have to find other resources. He has his right to his privacy," cautioned Dad.

TWO GRAMPS GOES MISSING

Two Gramps didn't answer his door when Billy Jack knocked on it Sunday morning. He knocked a second time but still no answer. He ran home and reported to Dad.

Dad said, "He often goes to visit his sister in Two Pines. He'll be back soon."

"But I really need to talk to him, Dad. We have to start on our reports tomorrow," cried Billy Jack.

"Then you need to do some research in your history book. If not on code talkers then on two-way radios. Not everybody relied on code talkers alone, I don't think. Or did you even remember to bring your history book home? Your *Ita* said you were pretty upset when you came home Friday."

Billy Jack thought for a moment. He remembered he waited in the hall at the school house after the other students left so he could ask Miss Gorman if he and Isaiah could trade topics. As he stood at the classroom door, he heard Isaiah ask her about the report and she said no, she had thought long and hard about each person before assigning certain topics. He had run out of the school house and for the bus until Isaiah stopped him. He had yelled at Isaiah, was too angry to speak to anyone else. BUT NOW . . . HE HAD SECRET INFORMATION . . . that is if Two Gramps wanted to talk about it.

Maybe that's what Principal Grayson meant when he said something about someone sitting on his door step. Did he know his Two Gramps had been a code talker? How would he know?

"Well, did you, bring your school books home, Billy Jack?" reminded Dad.

"Uh, no, sir. I forgot them. Guess I'll have to ask Betty if I can borrow hers," admitted Billy Jack.

"Think she'll let you after what you did to her book and papers?" asked Mama with a smile.

Billy Jack went in search of his sister.

"I sure hope Two Gramps is willing to talk about it," whispered mama to dad.

Dad just shrugged his shoulders. "I wish now we hadn't read that letter out loud. Two Gramps may not even want to talk about it ever. I've heard it was really hard over there for the men and women."

"I know the women worked in the factories, but did they actually fight in the war?" asked Mama.

"Didn't you say Betty's report is on how the women served in the service? I guess we'll just have to wait to see what her report says," replied dad.

Billy Jack came home after looking for Isaiah, again his head hung down. "I wish I hadn't been so mean to Isaiah," he said to no one in particular. "Two Gramps isn't home and Isaiah won't come out so I can ask him if he knows his uncle and Two Gramps were code talkers."

"Did you get a chance to apologize to him?"

"No," he said sitting at the table. Mama watched him. She knew he was feeling badly about his treatment of Isaiah. Besides she knew he really wanted to tell his friend about Two Gramps and his uncle. Watching him Mama knew he thought he was too old to cry so he held his tears back. She glanced out the window and saw Isaiah throwing the ball against his grandma's house. Knowing his mother would soon be out to scold him for making noise she said, "Billy Jack, if you want to save Isaiah from a scolding from his *Ita*, go over and play catch with him."

Billy Jack just sat there.

"Oh no, you are too late. I see her through the window and she is heading to the door. Poor kid." She shook her head, a small smile on her face as she watched Billy Jack jump up and race out the door. She didn't even remind him 'no running in the house'.

"Isaiah, throw me the ball, quick," he called to his friend.

Isaiah turned around and hurled the ball at Billy Jack. Then they moved away from the house to the open patch they called their playground, even though it was just a dusty, rocky square of ground. As they walked toward it Billy Jack put out his hand and Isaiah took it and shook. Friends again. Billy Jack sighed a big sigh of relief.

"Isaiah, I'm sorry. I know it wasn't your fault you got the report I wanted and I got the report you wanted," said Billy Jack. He heard a snicker and looked at Isaiah. He was laughing. Billy Jack started to get angry all over again thinking Isaiah thought it was all a big joke. But Isaiah had fallen to the ground and was really laughing. Billy Jack just stared at him.

"Billy Jack, don't you think it's funny? We were both so sure we would get what we wanted and neither one of us did." Isaiah asked still laughing.

Mama was right. Isaiah was a special friend. Billy Jack dropped to the ground too and started laughing. Soon they heard mothers calling their kids in for supper. Billy Jack sat up. Remembering Mama's rule about apologizing no matter how much it hurt to say the words, Billy Jack said, "Isaiah Gibson, I'm sorry I yelled at you. I wanted to tell you about the letter Two Gramps got from the government saying that he is to be honored because he was a code talker in World War II. He isn't even Navaho. I guess that's why Miss Gorman gave me the report on communications. I sure hope he remembers something. It was a long time ago, you know, and he is old." He stood up and started to go then said, "I wonder how she knew about it, and Mama and Dad didn't. Oh, and I was going to tell you, too, if I had found out Two Gramps served at the Battle of Dunkirk, I would have told you so you could interview him."

"Thanks, Billy Jack. I have to apologize to your mother, I was rude to her. I'm glad we are friends again. See you tomorrow," said Isaiah as he started to run off to the sound of his mother calling.

Isaiah stopped and turned back. "Billy Jack, I asked my grandma if we look at the booklet about her brother and she said yes but to handle it with great care as it is history of our tribe. So one of these days we will look at it together. I wish my great uncle had lived so we could listen to the two men talk about being code talkers. See ya."

***

BETTY VISITS MRS. LITTLE DEER

Betty sat at the kitchen with a stack of encyclopedias and old history books. "Mama, did the women wear uniforms and go with the men to fight?"

"I really don't know, Betty. Nowadays the women are trained to handle weapons, but I don't think they did 60 years ago. What does your history book or encyclopedia say?" asked Mama.

"It doesn't say anything about them shooting guns," said Betty frowning.

"How about the school computers. Do you know how to find what you need to know on a computer?"

"No, but it doesn't really matter because it seems like whenever I go to the computer someone is there already. That's why I brought all of Dad's old encyclopedias and history books from the storeroom. I hope he doesn't care if I use them. But they really don't talk anything except the battles."

"No, he won't care as long as you are careful and put them away after you are through with them. I remember I didn't get much out of the war lessons but girls really aren't interested in wars, you know."

"I agree", sighed Betty thumbing through an old book.

Billy Jack came into the house.

"Did you apologize to Isaiah?" asked Mama.

Billy Jack, remembering Isaiah rolling on the ground laughing, smiled and said, "Yeah, we're friends again."

Billy Jack sat at the kitchen table, with his math book, which he remembered to bring home after school, open in front of him but his mind was else where. Two Gramps still hadn't come back from his visit to his sister's home, so Billy Jack still hadn't asked him about being a code talker. Would Two Gramps remember any of it and would he talk about it? Billy Jack couldn't imagine just what was meant by code talking thus his mind slipped back to the stories Two Gramps had told about Chief Red Cloud. Billy Jack treasured the stories and the times he and his dad and other male relatives spent at an old campground listening to Two Gramps tell about his ancestors. Two Gramps was no longer able to walk to the campsite where he said Red Cloud chose to camp. He loved to hear Two Gramps tell the stories of the Lakota people using their natural language. He didn't understand all the words and found them hard to pronounce.

One of his favorite stories, was about smoke signals and Billy Jack loved stories of smoke signals. He wanted to learn more about them.

Billy Jack wished he could learn the language of the smoke signals. He did know that different tribes used different methods for creating the smoke. For instance, if they were near a stream or creek they could use wet grass to create the smudge, replacing the grass it as it dried from the heat. In the dry lands they would use wood from living trees called green wood.

The location of the signal fire was important, too. It was built at the highest point of a hill. If the signal came from half way up the hill it could suggest all was well but if it came from the top of the hill it signified danger.

The story of Chief Gray Eagle and his son Young Hawk was old, long before the people were moved on to the reservations. One day a runner came into Gray Eagle's camp late in the afternoon to deliver news of an attack on a nearby Lakota encampment where Gray Eagle's brother and family lived. Everything had been destroyed and a great many of the people had been killed. Gray Eagle gathered his family and four warriors and the family's belongings and set out not knowing how long they would be gone. The next morning, as they rose to prepare to continue the trip, Young Hawk heard his father call to him, "Son, arise, arise and greet the morning star," as he strode to the east and the rising sun. Young Hawk joined him while Mother prepared breakfast over the campfire.

Later Gray Eagle instructed his son, "Young Hawk, you will watch for the smoke signal I will send when I find and kill a buffalo. You will bring your mother to prepare the meat for travel. With so many of the men in Many Kills camp killed the survivors are in need of food and hides to feed and clothe their families. Whatever we bring will be welcomed."

As Father rode out Young Hawk saw three of the four warriors ride forward and join him. Looking for the fourth warrior he saw him step out from behind a tree a rifle held across his chest. Young Hawk, content all was well, pulled a small piece of flint from his par fleche tied at his waist and began chipping at it glancing at the sky from time to time. Nearby mother sat sewing a small shirt as she too, watched the horizon. The messenger had reported Gray Eagle's brother and wife were among those killed leaving small children."

He was glad his dad had translated it for him so they could both enjoy the story.

Boy, just to be responsible for watching for the smoke signal!! Billy Jack wished he knew more about smoke signals. Maybe one day Two Gramps would take time to explain it to him. He could just see himself and Two Gramps on Horsehide Hill sending smoke signals to warn the tribe of the enemy approaching . . .

A sharp knock on the screen door brought him out of his dream world.

"Billy Jack, are you finished doing your math problems yet? Your mom said you could come out and play kick ball with us if you are," called Isaiah through the screen door

Billy Jack looked at the page number of his book and then flipped to the last page of the chapter. Darn, he thought I've only read one page and have five to go.

"Give me about 5 minutes and I will be finished. The last few pages have lots of pictures on them."

"Well, hurry up or it will be time for the rest of us to go home for supper," replied Isaiah before running off the porch. "Sorry guys, he must have been day dreaming about his ancestor Red Cloud again instead of doing his math. You would think he would learn . . ." and then he was out of earshot for Billy Jack to hear what Isaiah was telling their friends.

Billy Jack wished he could think of life in the present instead of the past. But life had to be so much more interesting when the warriors raced across the plains. Nowadays the men went to work in factories, hospitals or ranches and farms. He couldn't even think of anything exciting his dad or grandpa had done. They had all stayed on the Rez and did what they needed to do to support their families

"Billy Jack, I don't suppose you finished your math problems yet have you? Well, go outside and play with your friends until supper. You need the fresh air. I'll help you after supper and check to see you got the right answers. Maybe if we do them together you can concentrate on them. I know you crave excitement in your life, and you find it in the stories Two Gramps used to tell you. But that school work has to be done."

Betty sat at the kitchen table, her notebook open but she wasn't writing. She was crying quietly. Tears rolled down her face. Several days had passed since she had first gone through all her dad's old history books and encyclopedias for information on what women did in the war. She knew about Rosie the Riveter, the name given to the women who put screws in airplanes. She wasn't quite sure just what that meant but not one had said anything about what else the women had done, let alone what a Lakota woman may have done. The books didn't even mention anything about women being nurses. Two Gramps said something about women in war but . . . if she could just get to use a computer!! The tears flowed again.

Mama walked into the kitchen and glanced at her then stopped and put her hand on Betty's shoulder. "Betty, what's wrong? Are you hurt?" she asked

Betty shook her head. "No, Mama," she answered.

"Are you sick?"

Again Betty shook her head.

"What's wrong then ?" Mama asked sitting beside Betty.

"I'm going . . . to . . . . get . . . an F on my History report," said Betty as she hiccupped from crying. "I've . . . never . . . had . . . had an F . . . on any of my scho . . . school work," she wailed.

"Betty, calm down. Now tell me. Billy Jack said the reports aren't due until next week so how can you get an F? You didn't turn in your report early and unfinished, did you?"

"No, that's what's wrong. I don't have a report. Well, I have this," she pushed a written paper toward her mother. Mama read *Women in World War II by Betty.*

The women took care of their families so their husbands could go to fight in the war. Some of them women worked in hospitals. Some of them worked in airplane factories.

"It really doesn't say anything about the women being in the service. Today in school every time I had my work done and went to a computer to work, someone else was there."

"Oh, I see what you mean. I thought Ginger was going to help you. Didn't she say her dad's aunt drove a jeep for a General?"

"Yes, but she's not Lakota so I couldn't interview her for the part that we were to interview someone who served from the Lakota people. And . . . and . . . besides, she died," said Betty beginning to cry again.

"Betty, stop. Stop. We'll work this out."

"But I have to have it ready to hand in a sum... sum..."

"A summary," helped Mama

"Yes, a summary on Monday and you have to work this weekend and Dad and Billy Jack are going to get Two Gramps and..."

"Okay, I get the picture. But I don't have to go to work this weekend as Mrs. Bad Elk had to go to the hospital so I don't have to clean her house until Monday. Now let's see what we can do," she exclaimed as she looked around.

"Oh, here it is. Remember when Isaiah brought over the papers his grandmother wrote about her brother when he was in the army? I've been reading them and discovered she also wrote about a friend of hers. Here you read it while I fix supper, and we will work on it tomorrow."

Betty was all smiles at the breakfast table the next morning. "Mama, the papers you gave me to read were really good, but I really need to talk to someone."

"I'll walk over and talk to Isaiah's mother and ask if his grandmother, Mrs. Little Deer is well enough to visit with you about her friend. Maybe we can go over later this morning. Get your breakfast eaten and your room straightened up, so if she is well enough we can go."

Later Betty and Mama walked over to Mrs. Little Deer's home. After the customary greeting to the old Lakota woman, Betty and her mother were invited to sit beside her bed.

"Elizabeth and Betty, it is so good to see you," said Mrs. Little Deer. "I am happy to tell you the story of my friend, Jeanette Little Finger. She and I were childhood friends. We both came from very poor families, but her family was even poorer than mine. She was very smart and determined to get off the reservation . . ."

Betty listened closely to Mrs. Little Deer and wrote things down so she would remember. Suddenly Mrs. Little Deer stopped talking. Betty looked at the elderly woman afraid she had gotten too tired to talk anymore, but saw that Mrs. Little Deer was thinking real hard.

"I remember she joined a group of women in the Air Force that had a special name; bumble bees or dragon flies or some insect. When it was disbanded, she joined the Air Force Reserves and was highly ranked. She received many medals of honor." She sat silently for a moment and then said, "Oh, I remember she was a WASP."

Mrs. Little Deer settled back in her bed with a sigh. Mama took Mrs. Little Deer's hand. "Thank you so much for your story. We, too, are proud of your friend. When Betty writes about her it will be the best she can do," promised Mama as she stepped back away from the bed.

Betty stood beside the bed. "Thank you so much, Mrs. Little Deer. It will be the best report turned in, I think," she said before turning away. She started to follow her mother then turned back around. "I hope I didn't make you too tired."

Mrs. Little Deer smiled. "No, I never tire when I can tell of my special friend. Thank you, for letting me share her story. I would like to hear your report when you have finished it."

Betty looked at her mother. Mama smiled. "Of course, Mrs. Little Deer, I would be proud to read it to you. Thank you, again," said Betty as she followed her mother out the door.

Betty was all smiles when she went home. She could write her report, and it would be a good one. Billy Jack was sitting on the front steps of their house when Mama and Betty got home. He and dad had brought Two Gramps home from Two Pines.

"I see you and Dad are home. Did you get a chance to talk to Two Gramps about your report?" asked Mama.

"No, I wanted to wait until I could sit and talk to him and write down things. Then after we got home, Mr. Jefferson brought him a message, then this man came. I think he and the man left. I've been sitting here watching. He didn't light his kerosene lamp in the kitchen. Well, I guess I'll go over and knock again just in case he is in the bedroom," sighed Billy Jack. Getting up to go to Two Gramps house. After Billy Jack knocked on the door he waited for Two Gramps to invite him in but no one did.

The next morning when the school bell rang, Betty was afraid what Miss Gorman would say when she had to admit that Mama helped her with her report. Of course Billy Jack would have to admit he had help when they found out Two Gramps had been a code talker. But that was different.

"Children," Miss Gorman clapped her hands to gain their attention. "That's better," she said when they had settled down. After the salute to the flag Miss Gorman turned to the class and said, "I have heard some of you talking. It seems to me you are of the opinion that the Lakota fought the war and won it all by themselves. That's my fault and I apologize. Yes, Daniel?'

"You did say we were to write only about the Lakota," he commented.

"Okay, let me ask you, how many of you have found a Lakota family member or friend to talk about their part in the war?" Miss Gorman saw five hands raised and counted them out loud, "1 . . . 2 . . . 3 . . . 4 . . . 5 . . . Only five. How could only five men win a war?

"According to one source I found, 44,000 American Indians served in World War II but even that many would not have been enough to overcome the enemy," Miss Gorman continued. "Let's get back to why I suggested only Lakota. The majority of this class have Lakota ancestors and I want you to come to know them through your report. If you are of another tribe and your ancestors fought in World War II or know of somebody of a different tribe by all means use that source. Remember no matter what your ancestry is, you may all be proud someone cared enough to sign up to fight for our country. Pride is an uplifting feeling if you don't let it tip you upside down and embarrass you. Now who has questions?"

Billy Jack raised his hand she nodded to him. "Not all of us have had a chance to talk to everyone in the family."

"So your summary isn't ready?" asked Miss Gorman.

Billy Jack shook his head. "My Two Gramps went to visit his sister. I know he was in the war as he got a letter from the government . . ." Billy Jack stopped short. What if Two Gramps didn't remember anything or didn't want anyone to know about his business.

Betty raised her hand.

"Yes, Betty."

"I'm supposed to write about the women in the war. My mama and I visited Mrs. Little Deer. Is that alright, I mean Mama asking Mrs. Little Deer about her friend who was a WASP or do I have to find someone on my own?" asked Betty hoping Miss Gorman would let her use her information.

"Again, I apologize, I didn't realize how few living sources we have to give us a full picture. Nor was I aware of how much information has been put on the computer that you have to go to several sites to find out about one thing. It never seems to stop with just one or two articles on each subject. You have less computer user knowledge than I expected, so if you know of any adult with computer knowledge who offers to help you look or who has a story to tell accept their help."

Isaiah, was given permission to speak next. "I'm glad you said that. I looked on the internet and found so many references I didn't have time to read them all. I kind of messed up my friend's computer, because I forgot to log out before I started to look at another one."

Ginger raised her hand, she saw Miss Gorman nod at her. "I am to write about what the civilians did. Dad is gone this week and I asked Betty's mom for help. Mrs. Bladen said she heard that not many people living on the rez had radios or newspapers so they really didn't know what was going on except when a neighbor boy was killed or missing in action. Most people couldn't afford to buy newspapers back then, so they didn't know what the army and navy were doing. Oh, Dad did give me his Orange book to read and it told about collecting scrap iron, whatever that is, and one boy won a prize for collecting the biggest piece. He found an old farm plow in the corner of a barn nobody ever used. But Miss Gorman, how could the soldiers or sailors use a plow?" Especially without a horse and where would they get a horse over there? I hope Dad comes back soon so I can see if he knows anything."

Miss Gorman laughed. "I'm sure he does or knows where to find it. Okay, class your questions have proven what I was beginning to wonder. New rules. You may ask anyone you want to help look up information you need. Most of you have not used the computer enough to know how to get the most out of what it has to offer. With this extra help though, I think we should still make the essays start at no less than 75 words with the same restrictions: no counting *ifs, and, the, or or buts.* Please add these questions to your list of instructions.

1. What years did the war take place?

2. Where was it fought?

3. When did the Americans join it?

4. How many different countries were in the war?

5. What were the names of the two groups fighting?

6. Name at least two officers on each side.

After you have those all written down take out your history books and look them up. You have the rest of the class period to find as many as you can. We will discuss the answers tomorrow. If you don't finish, take your book and notebooks home with you. If an adult asks to help, let them."

Billy Jack knocked on Two Gramps door again after school on Monday and still no answer. After no answer on the second time he knocked Billy Jack ran home and reported to his dad.

"I'm sorry Billy Jack. I'm a little concerned, too. He must have decided to go visit someone else after we brought him home."

"But I really need to talk to him, Dad. We have to start on our reports," cried Billy Jack.

"Then you need to do some research in your history book. Like I said the other day, if not on code talkers then on two-way radios."

"That was last Friday. Miss Gorman gave us some new questions to look up and add to the report. I'll look those up now." Billy Jack went in search of his book and assignment.

The children continued to work on their reports. Often there would be a soft knock on the classroom door and then an older Indian person would walk in and go to a table and sit to wait for their child or grandchild to join them. Together they would open a book or go to a computer and begin working on a report. Miss Gorman would smile at the newcomer and go on teaching what ever class she was working with.

The closer the 'big day' came for the fourth graders, he more visitors came in and out.Then it was here!! Today, Friday, October 12, had arrived. Miss Gorman led the class in the Pledge of Allegiance then started the music for The Star Spangled Banner. Jericho had sat down and quickly jumped up and joined in.

When the song ended, Miss Gorman motioned for them to sit and asked, "What day is today?"

Many voices called out, "Report day!" "Our special gathering." "Our talks for our guests." "The day Columbus discovered America in 1492."

But one voice was loudest of all, "My birthday!!"

Miss Gorman looked surprised. "That's right Jericho. It is your birthday. I guess in all the excitement I forgot. Boys and girls stand and sing Happy Birthday to Jericho."

After the singing and everyone was settled Miss Gorman said, "I heard someone say it was Columbus Day."

"That's right, Columbus discovered America on my birthday!"

The children burst out laughing. Miss Gorman waited until they were quiet then said, "A good math problem. If Jericho was born on the day America was discovered how old would he be?"

The papers and pencils flew and finally a voice called out," "510".

"Very well done, Fredrick. But I think we will just wish Jericho a happy eleventh birthday and get ready for our program. The parents, grandparents and guests will begin arriving in about 2 hours. In the meantime we will continue with our daily lesson until they arrive. When Mrs. Proctor, our new principal, tells us they are ready for us I will remind you of your last minute instructions before we go out.

"Yes, Betty, you have a question?"

"Will Mr. Grayson and Ginger be here?" asked Betty.

"The last I heard from them they planned to be here,." said Miss Gorman.

"I hope so," whispered Betty wiping her eyes.

The children were busy until a double knock on the door alerted them the audience had gathered and were waiting for them. They each placed their book, pencil and note books in their desks, took out a bound booklet and stood by their desks.

"Okay, Class, this is it. Please remember how hard you each have worked. Let us quietly join our guests. Robert is your leader today, so he will lead you to your row of chairs which are marked." She nodded to Robert who nodded back, "When you get there, sit down, have your report pages in correct order and keep them quiet. When the last speaker has left the stage on the left side you enter on the right and go to the microphone, ask your guest who helped you to join you. If they decline, introduce them by name and then begin your report. Isaiah will be our first speaker and he will answer all of the questions you were to answer so each of you doesn't have to share that information but it will help the audience understand your report better. If a certain officer was mentioned in your report share it as not all officers were at all battles. Is that clear?"

"What if we forget when it's our turn and read it anyway?" asked Betty.

"If you forget and read it don't worry about it. Just continue reading. Are you ready?"

"Yes, Miss Gorman," came a quiet reply. Miss Gorman smiled at them, nodded for Robert to begin the trek to the gathering room. She stopped Todd who was behind Betty and quietly said, "Leave a chair empty between you and Betty for Ginger." Todd nodded and followed Betty to the auditorium.

Betty looked back at Miss Gorman who stood with her head bowed. She smiled. They would do well as Miss Gorman had asked a blessing on them. She followed Jericho wishing it were Ginger in front of her.

Miss Gorman went to the microphone and welcomed the people. "Every year the 4th and 5th grade class study the story of America's struggles for freedom. This term it was World War II against the big powers called the Axis. Because of the sudden recognition of some of our tribal members who fought in that war, our former principal suggested they study in depth what the Lakota people and all American

Indians contributed to the war. Each 4th grade student was assigned a special topic to report on. It was their responsibility to find as much information as they could about an American Indian who served in some way. Today the students will share their information with you. Isaiah are you ready?" asked Miss Gorman.

Isaiah stood but didn't begin his walk to the stage. "Well, I was hoping my dad would be here." he said looking around. He waited then went to the podium. "He just got home a couple of days ago." Isaiah continued as he settled his booklet on the podium.

"When I told him about our history report he didn't seem too interested, but then I noticed some notes he had added to my folder. Mom said he had remembered some things his grandpa had told him about being overseas after the Americans joined the fight. One story he remembered was that his grandpa met a British soldier and they had become friends. The man said he and some of his troops were waiting on the shore watching as other men farther down were being rescued by men coming across the channel in small boats. They waited hoping one of them would come to where they were. Suddenly one came their way. The driver waited in the boat until he saw couple of soldiers trying to help a wounded man into the boat so he got out of his boat and went up the nearby sand dune to help. When he noticed a band of German soldiers coming over a sand dune behind them he knew he and the other men couldn't make it back to the boat in time so the driver waved to the ones in the boat to go. Dad's grandpa' . . . Hey, that would be my great grandpa wouldn't it? Anyway, my great grandpa's friend had to drive the small boat from the shore to one of the larger ships waiting farther out in the channel. The drivers of all the small boats were hurrying to save as many men as they could so after the boat was full the men in the boat just kept yelling. "Let's go, Let's go," so the British man said he just drove it like he would have his tank. And they made it to a larger boat just as thousands of others had in the five days the rescue had gone on. Dad said he remembered the story because he thought the fact that the man was from the Island . . . no, that's not right . . . It wasn't island . . .

"Isle of Man," came a deep voice from the doorway.

"Oh, yeah, Isle, yeah, the man was from the Isle of Man. Miss Gorman, this my dad, Joseph. Now I am ready to begin my report."

Miss Gorman walked over to Joseph, shook his hand, and watched as he walked up the steps to join his son at the podium.

"You really look nice, Dad. Thank you for coming," said Isaiah quietly to his dad.

Then turning to his classmates and families attending he said, "My report is on the Battle of Dunkirk in France. The exciting and interesting thing about this battle is the rescue of thousands of men from the enemy."

THE BATTLE OF DUNKIRK

World War II started in 1939 when Germany began threatening Poland, and it was fought in Europe. The Americans joined it in 1944 after Japan attacked Pearl Harbor in Hawaii. There were two groups. One group was called the Axis and they were Russia, Germany and Italy. The Allies were nearly all the other countries of the world including the United States.

The computer listed fifty three countries as Allies, three as Axis and eleven didn't join in the fight. The Axis leaders were Adolf Hitler of Germany, Hirohito of Japan and Benito Mussolini of Italy. For the Allies the three main leaders were Franklin Roosevelt of United States, British Prime Minister Winston Churchill and Josef Stalin of Russia.

France and the United Kingdom, Britain and Northern Ireland declared war against Germany in 1939 but fighting didn't start until 1940. This was before the Americans joined in the fight so there were no Lakota men fighting in this battle. Since the Americans weren't in the war at that time, I can't name two American officers, but the French General of the Supreme Allied Commander, Maurice Gamelan, was the commanding officer for the Allies.

German soldiers marched across France until they had driven the Allied soldiers to the English Channel. Germany's air force attacked, then their tanks came, and it wasn't long before they had France beaten.

Before Germany could overrun France and capture the beaten soldiers, the people of France and countries around them made a mighty rescue. France couldn't defend her land so the people surrendered. That left thousands of servicemen from Britain, France and Belgium to be captured by the enemy.

Messages about the men being captured or pushed into the sea were sent to people of the surrounding countries and boats from those countries came to save them. About one thousand British boats came. There were all kinds of boats. Fishing boats, rich people's fun boats: "My dad said those were called Yoks." Isaiah stumbled over the word. Looked at his dad. Joseph smiled and said, "YACHTS."

Yachts and tug boats. "Dad said those are the little boats that pull big ships into port." Isaiah looked down at his paper and continued reading, *and little motor boats.*

They saved over 300,000 men in five day, but a lot of men were not saved. They were taken prisoners. Almost all their fighting equipment had to be left behind

Isaiah bowed to his audience. He and his father started to leave the stage when he noticed Miss Gorman come forward, and he stopped. His dad continued to his chair and sat down.

"Isaiah, where did you find the information?" asked Miss Gorman coming forward.

"My mom works in an office. She knew how to run the computer so we came to the school and got the information. I didn't understand why I had to write about it when no Lakota were in the battle," said Isaiah.

"Do you remember when Mr. Grayson spoke to us when we first started this lesson? He said he enjoyed this story because it told of how men of many countries worked together to save thousands of people? That's what he wants all of us to learn."

"Working together we can do anything. I find it very interesting of all the students to give reports, you would have a connection to this battle even though it was a very small connection. Neither of us knew it until after you got started. Thank you, Mr. Gibson, for helping Isaiah to include the interesting fact about the boat driver. Isaiah, part of the assignment was to include any new words you learned. Do you have some?" asked Miss Gorman.

"Did I ever!" exclaimed Isaiah. Going to the large portable blackboard he wrote down blitzkrieg, Luftwaffe, panzerwagen and Wehrmacht. Turning to the audience and using the teacher's long pointer he explained what the words meant.

"Wehrmacht is the same as our saying Armed Forces; the army, air force and navy all together. Blitzkrieg meant a new type of fighting. It was like sending only the men who were the best shooters with all the guns and cannons at the enemy all at once.

My third word is luftwaffe and that means the German air force. My last word is panzerwagen. That meant their tanks and other army trucks that had extra steel on them to protect them from the enemy. Isaiah dusted the chalk off his hands. The audience clapped and clapped. Isaiah grinned and bowed then walked down and sat down.

Jerome stood at the microphone waiting for the audience to quiet down.

Battle of Iwo Jima

I was assigned to tell the story of Iwo Jima. It was a battle against Japan for an island in the Pacific Ocean north of the Marianna Islands. It was fought in late 1944 and early 1945 by the American Marines who were now part of the Allied forces. One reason the Americans wanted to capture the island was because the Japanese had a radio station on it for sending information seven hundred fifty miles north to their military headquarters in Japan. The incoming Allied planes were supposed to attack the 38 mainland of Japan but were attacked before they got to Japan because the Japanese were well ensconc . . .

Jerome stopped and looked at a lady who sat at the back of the auditorium. She didn't say anything and Jerome kept looking at her. Finally she stood up and came forward.

"Ensconced, Jerome." she said quietly.

"Oh, yeah, ensconced." He looked at Miss Gorman.

She was smiling. "I see that word is on your list of new words, Jerome. Maybe you had better explain it," said Miss Gorman.

Jerome looked again at the lady who had helped him. "My mother's friend who is visiting us is Pima Indian from Arizona. Her mother knew Ira Hayes when she was a child. I wanted her to come up here with me but she didn't want to." explained Jerome.

"We worked hard on that word, ensconced. It means 'well settled'," she explained.

Jerome returned to his paper.

The Japanese were ensconced and fortified because they had a network of bunkers. Bunkers are underground shelters on the island with hidden artillery.

The Allies fought hard for this island because they needed it to refuel and repair their fighter planes to attack mainland Japan.

They also needed to stop the radar the Japanese were using to report the Allied planes carrying fuel and bombs. The Allies were sure they could capture it as they had superior weapons and because the enemy could not retreat nor be quickly reinforced with fresh troops from Japan.

The most interesting fact about this battle was that after the Americans captured it, six men, five marines and one corpsman placed an American flag on top of Mount Suribachi. One of those men was Ira Hayes, a Pima Indian. A war photographer took a picture of the men and it became a very famous picture.

"Oh, yes. I only found the American officer on the internet in the article I read. He was Major Harry Schmidt of the Marine Corps."

"My mother's friend who helped me is Mrs. White Fang.'

Miss Gorman walked to Mrs. White Fang and shook her hand. Mrs. White Fang smiled at Jerome and walked back to her chair.

Jerome went to the blackboard and wrote. *ensconced* and *corpsman*. "These are the new words I learned. Ensconced means settled and corpsman means an enlisted man trained to give first aid or minor medical attention. Thank you." He bowed and left the stage.

Betty heard some of her classmates whispering but didn't turn around because Jerome was going off the left side of the stage and Fred had mounted on the right side and she was to go up after he was through so she had to think about that. Suddenly she felt someone's hand on hers. She looked up and let out a squeal.

"Ginger! You're back!" she cried when she looked up and saw Ginger looking down on her. Betty pulled Ginger down and gave her a big hug.

Miss Gorman frowned at Betty but smiled and Ginger.

"Welcome back Ginger. We'll be ready for your report soon. Fred is going to give his next," said Miss Gorman. "Fred."

Fred stood in front of the audience.

"I wanted to write about a battle but Miss Gorman had given all of them out she felt were important because she wasn't able to find Lakota in all the battles. Other battles were important and she hoped all would have a reference to the Lakota if possible. She explained the non-military people were just as important as the military in their own way, because what they did was to support the troops by doing certain things here at home. I didn't really have anyone help me. I learned how to use the computer and found lots of information."

He lifted up his papers and began to read.

How the People at Home Helped

The men went to war so the women had to go to work outside their homes to keep the businesses open and support their families. Before the war most women didn't work outside of their homes but took care of their kids and did the housework. Some of the women might have been nurses or dress sewers but they didn't go to business buildings to work to earn money as that was the dad's job. After the war started and the men left home, the women had to go to work to take the place of the men, in the hospitals, stores, barber shops, and all other types of business. The storekeeper's wife had to learn how to order groceries, clothing, shoes, and farm supplies for all their customers. Others had to learn how to drive cars or trucks. Some even drove tractors on farms. Some women had to learn how to put gas in the car, wash windshields, change oil, change and repair tires at a gas station. Back then when you went to a gas station, the man who worked there did all those things. Now the car owner does all that except repair the tire. The women also had to go to work in factories where war machines such as airplanes, jeeps and tanks were built. Cars were no longer built because the steel was needed in the factories for the war machines

At the beginning of the war, sugar and tires for cars and trucks were rationed. Which means your parents couldn't buy them without special stamps. Sugar and rubber were grown in other countries, and the men in other countries were fighting in the war or had no ships to send the goods to us. So our government made rulings that a person could only buy so much and use special stamps to buy them. Everywhere you went you could hear people talking about the "war effort" which really meant "don't complain! Just think of the men and women who are fighting in strange countries so we can live in the United States." Some of the other things that were rationed later in the war were gasoline, shoes, meat, laundry soap and flour. They were all needed by our men and women who were fighting the war. I didn't copy down all the things that were rationed," Jerome said to the audience. He looked at his paper again. The only way you could buy these things was with these special stamps. "Oh, and money, too." If you used up all the stamps you had, you had to wait until the next month to get more stamps from the government. Recipe books the moms used to see how to cook food had to be rewritten using less . . . lesser amounts or substitutes of the ingred . . . ingredients.

My mom said her great grandpa owned a general store. "She said it was like a small department store because it had everything," and great grandma had to count the stamps that came in everyday and send the information to the government every month.

She had seven children to take care of and all of her housework as well as counting the stamps correctly. It was hard for her. She would count so carefully before sending the information into the government and then she would often get a letter from the government saying she had miscounted. To do it over again. Grandma told Mom she often heard Great Grandma crying as she sat up late at night recounting the stamps. It was always late at night, after she had done her dishes and put her children to bed.

In order to keep things straight the government gave out different colored or marked stamps. Each person could buy only the amount of gas that his stamp said. If you were a truck driver your stamp had a T on it, X was for government people, R for farm tractors, B was such people that were war workers, doctors, ministers, mail carriers, and railroad workers as well as for all the other people for their everyday use.

A record was kept and if you had already bought the amount allotted you, you had to wait for the next months stamps to be mailed to you. You had to write your name on the front of the book and weren't supposed to borrow or trade stamps with anyone.

All families got a ration book for each of their children. This was the way the people of the United States were able to help their men and women who were fighting in the war.

"The new word I learned was rationed. Rationed means food and other items are allowed for people for a certain length of time. Thank you." He started walking across the stage but noticed Betty wasn't waiting on the right hand of the stage. He stopped and motioned for her to get up. She just stared at him and then realizing what he wanted she jumped to her feet dropped her folder from her lap. Ginger picked it up and handed it to her.

"Good luck, Betty," she said.

Betty took her folder and went up the steps to the stage. She walked to the podium and placed her folder on it.

Betty took her folder and went up the steps to the stage. She walked to the podium and placed her folder on it. She looked at her audience. "My mother helped me with my report. First we looked up stories in my dad's old history books and encyclopedias. Then we went on internet. Dad helped us with the internet. My report is:"

Did Women Fight In the War?

In 1945 22 million women were working in war industries building ships, airplanes, jeeps and tanks, guns, and bullet factories. They were nurses, clerks, mechanics, pharmacists, cooks, and photographers for the armed forces.

Those who were in the women's service could have been in the WAACs in 1942. It stood for Women's Army Auxiliary Corps. In 1943 they became WACs, Women Army Corp and served overseas. The Navy had WAVES, which meant Women Accepted for Volunteer Emergency Service. The Coast Guards had a service for the women known as SPARs. The Air Force had an service for women known as WASP which stood for Women's Air Force Pilots and the USMCWR stood for United States Marine Corp Women's Reserves which actually started during the war before World War II, in 1918.

During World War I, 300 women replaced 300 men so the men could go do the fighting. The women were never trained to fight in the front lines.

The woman I want to tell you about is Jeanette Little Finger, a Lakota who served in the armed services. She was a childhood friend of our neighbor Mrs. Little Deer.

They both came from very poor families. Jeanette was very smart and determined to get off the reservation. She would often wrap herself in any extra clothing or blankets even in sheets of newspapers under her clothing if she could find them so she could walk to school even on the coldest days. If the teacher didn't go to the school house because of the weather, Jeanette would go into the schoolhouse anyway and start a fire in the stove and read from the books. Most of them were so old they were out of date, but she didn't care.

She wanted to learn everything. She came from a very proud family so when Jeanette used the school's wood for herself she would always bring the same amount back the next day. Often she would be seen along the creek looking for tree branches. Her father and brothers would chop them for her and help her get them to the school. They were very honest and proud people.

The government program that promised the American Indians schooling was what she used to go to college, but it took her many years to graduate. After college she worked for the Army which was building military bases and airfields. That is where she learned about flying for women. She earned a pilot's license. When the WASPs disbanded, she joined the Air Force Reserves and held the rank of Captain. Later she became a control tower operator.

"No, women didn't carry guns in World War II or were found on the front lines as they are now, but they were part of all the services that the men were in. The new words I learned are all the names of the women's groups that served with the men. The word Corp means an organized subdivision of a military establishment. Mrs. Little Deer who told me about Jeanette Little Finger and because she is ill couldn't come today so I went to her house and read her my report. She was very happy that I asked for her help. Thank you."

As Betty went off the right side of the stage Ginger came up the steps on the left. She went to podium and laid her papers down. She faced the people who had befriended her when she and her father moved to the village. She never felt she wasn't one of them.

"Good afternoon. I don't have any Lakota ancestors who fought in World War II, in fact I don't have any Lakota ancestors at all!"

Laughter broke out.

"I will adopt you as my granddaughter," said Two Gramps with a smile.

"Thank you, sir. Then I would be Betty's cousin." More laughter.

Ginger saw Miss Gorman frowning. "But I need to read my report. Since I had no Lakota relative to talk to about their part in World War

II, Miss Gorman thought maybe other things the Americans did in general to help the men and women fighting overseas should be my topic. I got my information mostly from a book Dad calls his 'Orange' book. It's the story of his home town and has lots of neat information in it. One of the Lakota persons Dad met while we lived here remembers his family didn't live on the rez during the war years. He remembers how they talked about helping to find copper, iron, and rubber that was then sent to be reproduced into war machines. That was the only Lakota person I know of who remembered what was done off the reservation to help the war effort.

How Our Families Helped

By Ginger Grayson

People were urged to buy War or Savings Bonds and car owners had to buy Federal auto stamps. That money went to national defense. President Franklin Roosevelt ordered the entire United States to use year round daylight savings time during the war years to conserve fuel needed to produce electricity for the factories.

People were urged to become members of 'civil defense' meaning anyone sixteen years old to eighteen and those too old to go to war were to become local firemen to fill in for the men who went to war. They were also messengers, blowers of sirens which were to warn people to go to their bomb shelters in case of an enemy airplane attack, and spotters for possible enemy planes dropping bombs. At night they were to look for lights in homes of people who didn't hang the required black out curtains or were careless in hanging them, letting lights shine out of the windows past the shade. The shades were to be let down over the window at dusk so when someone turned a light on later it wouldn't reveal anyone at home.

I couldn't find out what they were made of to make them shut out the light unless it was just a heavier material than what our regular curtains are made of and it was black material.

Our families here in the mid west so far from the oceans probably didn't need them but to be a good citizen the rules must be followed. And Fines could be heavy if someone was caught not following the rules.

Ginger looked at the audience. "Dad said there were probably other jobs but he thought this would be enough about the civil defense." Looking down at her paper again she began to read.

They even got the younger children involved in the 'war effort'. All towns were expected to take part in the scrap iron and paper drives. That meant the kids, using their wagons, mom's garden wheel barrow or any other type of vehicle that had wheels, went looking for old unused iron such as discarded farm machinery. One time in Dad's town, the banks offered, as a prize, a war bond for the most scrap iron collected.

A war bond is a paper saying "in ten years or later if they gave the 'bond' back to the bank they will be given more money than they had paid for it." My dad's cousin won it because he found on his farm an old metal plow that was stored in the corner of a barn that had been abandoned.

Ginger looked at her audience. "I asked lots of people I know how could the soldiers and sailors use an old plow and everybody just said "well, just think about it."

Finally my Grandma Miller asked what my report was on and I told her mostly about getting scrap iron to make into ships and other war vehicles. And she said, "Well?" So I think that's what they did with it! They made it into new iron to build a ship. Back to my report," she said as the laughter died down.

Sometimes the businesses of the towns gave prizes for the most scrap iron, aluminum foil or newspapers brought in. In the town where my dad's family lived they had a iron scrap contest for almost a month long and 580,000 pounds of scrap iron was gathered. This one was not just the children because the people of the Methodist church gathered 51,055 pounds and the Lutheran church people gathered 50,885 pounds. They had another 'drive'. *This one was just for only one day. All the schools, businesses and county offices were closed.*

Farmers brought their trucks and trailers to haul all that was scrap items that had been gathered to the gathering pile. They did this for free for their contribution. By this time rubber was added to the list.

One day the children alone gathered 3000 pounds. A drive for copper and brass was done and a movie was shown at the theater. A piece of brass or copper was the same as a ticket. Children also gathered milk weed pods to be used in life jackets which saved the lives of many service men and women. They had war loan drives where men and women donated money to the war effort. The towns and cities didn't have just one drive but month after month they would have some type of drive to help the 'war effort'. Americans stood up and were counted because they could be counted on to serve their country wherever they were needed.

"I didn't really learn any new words except scrap which means small piece of something bigger and not usable like it is now, just if they can make it into something new. Thank you."

Ginger picked up her papers and walked off the stage and Joshua took her place.

He cleared his throat. "It is hard for my grandpa to walk up stairs so he will just stand up. He was the one who helped me with my report. My report is known as the Battle of the Bulge or the Ardennes Offensive."

"Grandpa's cousin Jude Black Elk was killed at that battle. Jude's best friend, who was fighting with him at that battle, came and talked to Grandpa's dad about the battle because before he died Jude asked his friend to tell the Black Elk family he was proud to fight and die for his country. We looked in all the old history books Miss Gorman and Mr. Grayson had and we found some on the computer because Grandpa forgot some of what he had been told."

Roselyn Ogden Miller

My Report on the Battle of the Bulge or

The Ardennes Offensive by Joshua Black Elk

And his Grandpa Jude Black Elk

This battle was one of the last battles of the war. It lasted from December, 1944, through January of 1945. The German leader, Hitler, planned it to be the winning battle for Axis which was his side.

The reason it was called the Battle of the Bulge is because looking at the map you can see in the country of Belgium where some of the battle was fought looks like it has a bulge in it.

Joshua turned to a large map on the wall behind him. He took a pointer and followed the dividing line between the two countries.

Isaiah told you in his report about the Battle of Dunkirk that took place in France. This battle was fought in France as well as Belgium and Luxembourg. He pointed to the two countries again. The Battle of Dunkirk was fought four years earlier, before America joined in the fighting.

The reason Hitler thought this would be the last battle was because he thought the soldiers of the other side, the Allies, were falling apart and would be easy to beat. It was winter and Christmas was coming. The land they fought on was hard to fight on. That's because it was a densely forested mountain region in Belgium, France and Luxembourg. That means it was mountainous with lots of trees

Hitler thought if the Axis surrounded the Allies army and cut off their supplies, they would surrender. The Allies had to do a lot of work to repair the deep water ports because the Germans had wrecked them as well as put mines in them to blow up any ships that came in to unload the men and supplies. The railroads, too, had been torn up. The Axis had a secret plan. They wore white clothing so they would look like the snow and be hard to see. Sort of like 'camo' today.

Another reason the Germans thought they would win is because they had men who dressed in American uniforms and spoke just like the American people because they had come to America to learn how to be "an American". They knew all the code words and what they stood for, stole jeeps the Allies drove, and used them to join the Allied forces. They mixed up road signs, gave wrong directions when asked, and destroyed the communication lines. Sort of like the Indians used to do with the telegraph lines here in South Dakota in the olden days.

They bom… bom…"

"Barded, bombarded," his grandpa said loud enough for Joshua to hear.

"Oh, yeah, bombarded, and that means, they kept shooting without stopping.

Some of the weapons they might have used were submachine guns, machine guns, sniper rifles, anti-tank weapons, flame throwers and hand grenades. The Allies had airplanes in defense. Because of the snow that kept falling, they couldn't fly, Hitler sent word to American Major General McAuliffe to surrender and the Major General sent a one word answer. "Nuts".

The snow stopped falling. The airplanes were able to fly, so the Americans could fight. At the end of the battle the Axis soldiers had no incoming supplies such as food, or gas so they began walking back to Germany. It was the biggest land battle in World War II.

We are to tell you about at least two officers. This battle had lots of important officers. Four of them were Generals. General George Patton, General George Montgomery, General Omar Bradley, and General Dwight Eisenhower. He later became a president of the United States.

"Oh, something else interesting I wanted to tell you was that the people of Belgium took the Allied soldiers into their homes and fed them. If they needed doctoring, they took care of them. They gave them a warm place to sleep, too.

"My new words were offensive which means attack and camouflage which the same as camo and that means to hide something by making it look the same as the surroundings, such as trees or snow, making things different from what you are looking at. Like putting tree branches on the tanks to make them look like a part of the forest.

Joshua walked across the stage, down the steps to his grandfather, and they walked to where his grandfather had been sitting. When his grandfather sat down Joshua went back to his seat.

Tommy standing at the podium looked at his grandmother who sat in the front row. She smiled at him. Tommy took a deep breath and motioned to his grandfather who stood beside him.

"My name is Tommy White Wolf and this is my Grandfather Thomas Breckenridge. He helped me with my report. Grandma helped, too. She gave Grandpa coffee and cookies and me milk and cookies; chocolate chip. Grandpa's uncle was on a navy ship at Midway Isle and was killed during World War II. Grandpa was too young to enlist but loved to get letters from his uncle about the war. The soldiers and sailors never got to say where they were or how the war was going in their letters but grandpa said it was fun to get a special envelope in the mail with his mane on it. We used the computer. Grandpa's daughter teaches computer science in a high school, so she helped us find lots of information. Grandpa can't remember the name of his uncle's ship so I will just tell you about the most decorated ship of the war and highest ranked leader.

Battle of Midway Island
Turning Point of World War II

By Tommy White Wolf and his great grandpa
Thomas Breckenridge

First of all, Midway Island is called an atoll. That is a coral island where the ocean comes up to make a lake in the middle of the island. Anyone who lives on an atoll has to live on the outer edges. Birds known as albatross live there. They are also known as the gooney bird. It liked to live there but was a nuisance to the navy men and the planes that landed their planes there to refuel. The men tried to scare the birds away. Then they captured them and moved them to other islands but the birds always came back until one day the men discovered the gooney birds didn't like pavement so they paved wherever they could.

"That's just some information I thought was interesting. It has nothing to do with the battle," explained Tommy smiling at his audience.

Midway Island was important to the Americans because it was a refueling stop for airplanes that flew over the Pacific Ocean and for the naval ships that protected that area from Japanese invasion.

Many American ships were in that area. The most decorated one was the USS Enterprise and one of the officers was Admiral Nimitz. There were 28 American ships and 185 Japanese ships. One ship I read about was 887 feet long. Grandpa and I figured out it was more than 2 football fields long. (Proud that his love for football gave him a deeper understanding of what size the ships were, Tommy smiled at his audience).

The island was between Japan and Hawaii and on December 7, 1941 when the Japanese bombed Hawaii they also hit Midway, but the military men based there were able to defend the island. That was considered the first victory of the war. Four months later they were again attacked and that became known as the Battle of Midway.

Realizing the Americans could easily attack Japan from Midway Island, the Japanese leaders planned an invasion of 5000 Japanese service men. The Japanese had lost some of their ships in the Battle of the Coral Sea so an early morning surprise attack was planned. It failed because the Americans had broken the secret code the Japanese used. The Japanese dive bombers, torpedo bombers and fighters started the attack. Not only was the Japanese secret code broken by the Americans, but the weather and airplane trouble stopped them from spotting the American attackers. Even with these problems the Japanese were able to bomb and damage the American airbase but the Americans fought back. Flying low they kept the Japanese fighter planes down and making the high flying ones that were diving down at the Japanese ships a surprise.

Because the Japanese planes were sitting on the ships ready to fly and fight, the gas lines for putting more fuel in the ships and planes, the bombs and torpedoes for fighting were all right out where the Americans could see them, not hidden away in their hangars. That made them easy targets. Three of the four attacking Japanese ships were sunk. The fourth ship caused damage to the American ship named the Yorktown which later sunk. When the battle was over Midway Isle was still occupied by the Americans.

"The new words I learned were atoll which is what Midway Island is. It is made of coral. Grandma and I looked up the word coral, and we finally decided it was the bony skeletons of animals from the ocean. The other new word was secret code. Billy Jack will explain about secret code to you later. The officers I read about in this battle were Admiral Chester Nimitz and Lt. Commander Edwin T. Layton. Thank you."

Tommy bowed to his audience, took a hold of his grandfather's arm and helped him down the steps. Billy Jack stood waiting at the top of the steps with Two Gramps.

When Tommy sat down Billy Jack and Two Gramps went to the podium.

BILLY JACK TELLS OF
TWO GRAMPS HISTORY

My name is William Johnson Bladen just like my Two Gramps . . . my great grandpa. He doesn't remember the name his *ita* chose for him. He was called Whistles Like the Wind most of his life until he was taken to a special school. He wants me to tell you about this school for it plays an important part of his becoming a code talker.

One day when Two Gramps was about five years old, two white men came to his father's camp. Two Gramps called Whistles Like the Wind and five other boys just older than he were loaded in a large wagon pulled by a team of white horses. They were taken to a white man's town to the railroad. There they were placed in a railroad car. He huddled with the older boys on the floor leaning against a long bench. None of the white men spoke the Lakota language clearly. One man tried but the boys could not understand him They didn't know what was going to happen to them. Whistles Like the Winds father had told him all the boys were going for a long ride on an 'iron horse' and he was to obey his elders wherever he went just as he obeyed at home. Whistles Like the Wind nor any of the other boys had ever seen nor heard a train before.

The puffing noise of the engine and the piercing whistle frightened them even more.

As they traveled they became hungry. When one of the men brought them food, it didn't look like any food they had ever eaten, so they just left it on the plates. They rode for many hours without eating and when the man brought the food back to them they ate. They were too hungry to say no.

They didn't know how to relieve themselves on the train and it never stopped so they could get off. The man who tried to talk their language kept encouraging the boys to go with him past the seats to the end of the car but they were afraid they might get thrown out a door or window so they just sat with their heads down not looking at him.

Finally Whistles Like the Wind was so miserable that when the man came again and tried to show and explain what he wanted Whistles Like the Wind got up and followed him even though he was the youngest of the group. After he came back he had a big grin on his face and encouraged the others to follow the man. After that they were more trusting.

The train finally stopped. No longer were they in a land with large evergreen trees on hillsides but endless tall grass blowing in the wind across a flat land. As they looked around they saw no teepees or log cabins. "What now?" they asked each other. The man who tried to speak their language motioned for Whistles Like the Wind to follow him.

Afraid not to for there was no other place to go, Whistles Like the Wind followed the man with the boys following him. They walked a long time until they came to a stairway going up and three steps going down on the other side. It had no walls around it, just two poles holding up a sign. Again the white man tried to explain but again it made no sense to the boys. A year later when Whistles Like the Wind had learned to read the white man's words he saw that the sign said Green Valley Indian School.

In the days that followed, the children were told through an interpreter who spoke their language fluently they could no longer speak in their own language. They had to learn the white man's language. If they were caught they had their mouths washed out with a strong soap This was done, they were told by the interpreter, to wash away the old language so their mouths would be filled with only the white man's language. Eventually it was easier to say the new words out loud but they kept their language in their heart and head. Often when nobody was around, they would whisper the words so they would never forget them. But as time passed the old language left their minds and hearts.

They, who had run and rode their ponies in nothing more than a deer skin breech cloth, were suddenly told they must wear woolen shirts and pants. Heavy boots were made for their feet. Feet that had never worn any more than light moccasins. The hair of both boys and girls was cut short. It no longer brushed the back of their necks nor could be braided in the traditional manner.

Billy Jack paused as if to catch his breath and said, "Two Gramps wants me to tell you why at age five his father let him be taken to that far away frightening place. His father Black Bull saw the old ways disappearing with the coming of the 'white eyes.' That is why he let his small son go even though he was afraid for him, because of the stories he had heard about the schools. He hoped by learning the 'white eyes' ways Whistles Like the Wind would not only survive the new way of life, but that he would be of help to those who came later. The boy's mother mourned him as though he were dead."

"Like all the other children, Whistles Like the Wind was given a new name. A white man's name, William Johnson Bladen. A list of five names was written on the chalk board. The child was to choose one after the teacher read them out loud. After Whistles Like the Wind had stood in front of the black board for a long time, the teacher gave him a pointer and motioned for him to point to the name he wanted. Since he could only reach as high as the last name he hit it with the pointer. The teacher wrote it down in a book. Then on a piece of cardboard which he pinned to Whistles Like the Wind's shirt. The interpreter explained to the children that every morning after they put their uniform jacket on the name tag must be pinned to it. He would no longer be called Whistles Like the Wind. He must answer whenever the teacher called him William. It was so hard for one so small so the older boys helped him when they could by whistling a short note when they heard the teacher say William. But William sounded like Whistles so it wasn't long before he recognized his new name, William.

When he was ten years old he was put on a train again and sent home. He had a terrible time at home as he had had at school because he had almost forgotten the native words. But at least no one washed his mouth out with soap. No one in the village had learned the 'white eyes' language. The children treated him like he was an alien and wouldn't play with him, until one day a boy and his family moved into the village.

With great patience the new boy began to re-teach William the old language. Soon they were friends. Later Will and Two Kills went to a nearby white man's school for the Indian children and Will helped his new friend Two Kills learn the white man's way.

When they were older they enlisted in the army for World War II. Two Kills was given a white man's name, Henry Blackstone. One day not long after they had been sent to boot camp they were talking in their native language and Will noticed a white officer watching and listening to them. Remembering the punishment he had received during his early school days in the white man's school, he quickly switched to English and watched as the officer left the building. Later the same officer approached them and said they were to shower and dress in their best uniform as they were going to meet a Lieutenant General.

They didn't know what they had done that he to cause him to want to see them, but they did as they were told expecting the worst. After discussing their ability to speak and understand their native language with the Lt. General, they were sent to a room where other Lakota soldiers were creating a new language called a secret code. They did this by using the Indian words to explain: when, where and how gasoline and other supplies were being delivered for the troops; enemy troop movements; and other important information the Allied officers needed to know to direct the war. These were words that the Germans and Japanese did not understand. First the code talkers had to learn about each military item in the English, and then decide what word in Lakota best described that item. Since airplanes were an important part of war and the Lakota didn't have that word in their vocabulary they had to come up with an every day word that described it, such a "bird". Among the many words not in their native language were Officer, tank, jeep, machine gun, and bomb as well as others. They had to come up with an everyday word that described each item and now the Indian word for it.

Billy Jack stopped reading his report, grinned at Two Gramps, then at his audience and said, "No one had to whisper into the two way radio so the enemy wouldn't hear them. Even the American officers had to have someone interpret for them."

"Though only the Navaho tribe has been publicly honored, there were at least fifteen other American tribes in World War II and men of the Yankton Sioux transmitted messages during World War I."

"I looked through many sites on the computer but couldn't find the Lakota words used in the code. I did find lots of information on Navaho and a film on the computer that Two Gramps and I enjoyed watching together. The faces of these men are like ours rather than the white man's so it is easy for me to pretend they were our men. It reminded Two Gramps of his time there."

"I have some of the coded words in my essay to share with you, but first I want to tell you no American Indian code was ever broken by the enemy".

Billy Jack went to the chalk board and began writing. Two Gramps stepped to the microphone and said, "We used everyday words from our mother tongue such as turtle, tree, or horse. We had to learn all the names of the military equipment and how they were used. Such as mine sweepers, used to check for mines on land and in the water. We called them beaver. A 'half track' that looked like a truck in front and a tank in the back with no wheels but tracks made of heavy metal chains instead. We called one of those a race track. Officers like a Colonel was a silver bird. A fighter plane was called a humming bird. As he said each word in English he repeated it in his native tongue of Lakota.

Billy Jack came back and stood beside Two Gramps. He said, "These are just a few of the words they used. When a Japanese officer was told the secret to the secret code many years later, he thanked the person who told him. He said it had nearly driven him crazy trying to figure it out. I read in my research that the code talkers were warned never to talk about their job. The reports about them were classified and not to be known by the public. While in the war each code talker had a companion who guarded him against being captured by the enemy. The code talkers had heard that if they ever got captured the special soldier was to shoot him to protect the secret of the special code. I've met Two Gramps' special soldier. His name is Henry O'Neill.

"This past year the code talkers were invited to speak of their life as a code talker. I am very proud of my Great Grandpa William Johnson Bladen."

He smiled at Two Gramps and then turned to Mr. O'Neill. "Mr. O'Neill would you come up here with us?"

Two Gramps made room for Mr. O'Neill to stand beside him. Billy Jack turned to the two men and bowed. The audience stood and applauded. Billy Jack wiped tears of pride from his face and begin writing words on the black board with their double meanings.

ABOUT THE AUTHOR

Roselyn Ogden Miller through her love of children and children's stories has shared many hours reading to children of all ages. It was through this love that she first became interested in writings of the children who were placed on trains and sent hundreds of miles away from their natural families to find new homes and become part of a. family again in the two books POOR AS CHURCH MICE, Children of the Orphan Trains and POOR AS CHURCH MICE Book II.

Printed in the United States
By Bookmasters